The Night You Were Born

With love for Brenna and Haley,
two lights, shining, shining — W.R.M.

To Holly and Tess — S.W.

Orchard Books
96 Leonard Street, London EC2A 4XD
Orchard Books Australia
14 Mars Road, Lane Cove, NSW 2066
1 86039 870 7
First published in Great Britain in 1999

A CIP catalogue record for this book
is available from the British Library
2 4 6 8 10 9 7 5 3 1
Printed in Singapore

The Night You Were Born

Wendy McCormick

illustrated by Sophy Williams

ORCHARD BOOKS

The night that Jamie's sister was born,
Jamie was waiting for her at home,
all night long, all alone.

Well, he wasn't all alone,
Jamie's two cats were there,
sleeping on the window sills in the kitchen.

Oh, and Jamie's Aunt Isabel.
She was there, too,
washing up soup bowls from their dinner.

"Will Mummy and Daddy remember me,"
Jamie asked her,
"waiting here, all night long?"

"Of course, they will," Aunt Isabel said.
Then she told Jamie that waiting
was a big job, an important job.

“We have to light the way for this
new baby,” she said.
So they went to the front hall
and turned on the light
over the front door.

And they went to the back hall
and turned on the light over the back door.

"I waited for you, too, you know,"
Aunt Isabel said, "the night you were born."
"You did?" Jamie asked,
as he turned on the lights in the hall
and the two of them started upstairs.

"Yes," Aunt Isabel said.
"But you were so very late," she said.
"We waited and waited."

Aunt Isabel turned on the lights
in Jamie's room.
Jamie switched on his nightlight
shaped like a seashell.

"What did you do while you
waited for me?" he asked
while he made a pile of pillows on his bed.
"That's a long story," Aunt Isabel said
as they snuggled up with Jamie's two cats.

Jamie flipped on his torch
and he shone it on the ceiling.
"Where were you?" he asked.

"The night that you were born
I was far away from here," Aunt Isabel said.

"Your uncle and I were driving here to meet you.
We knew you were on your way, too,
but we weren't sure when you'd arrive."

"That morning had been the foggiest morning we'd ever seen.
'Is this the day?' I thought, as the fog settled around us
thick as a nest of furry rabbits.
'The day that he'll be born?'"

"Was it the day?" Jamie asked.
Aunt Isabel kissed the top of Jamie's head.
"You'll see," she said.

"We phoned the hospital from the misted road.
'Is today the day?' I asked.
'We don't know yet,' they told me.
'Nothing yet,' I said to your uncle."

"I was very late," Jamie told Aunt Isabel.
"Very," Aunt Isabel said as she began again.

"Then, as the mist rose, we drove on, along the tip of a narrow spiny wing of land, past fields mounded with clover and daisies, past fishing villages tucked into tiny inlets all of them leaning outward, as if they were waiting, too, just like me for word about you."

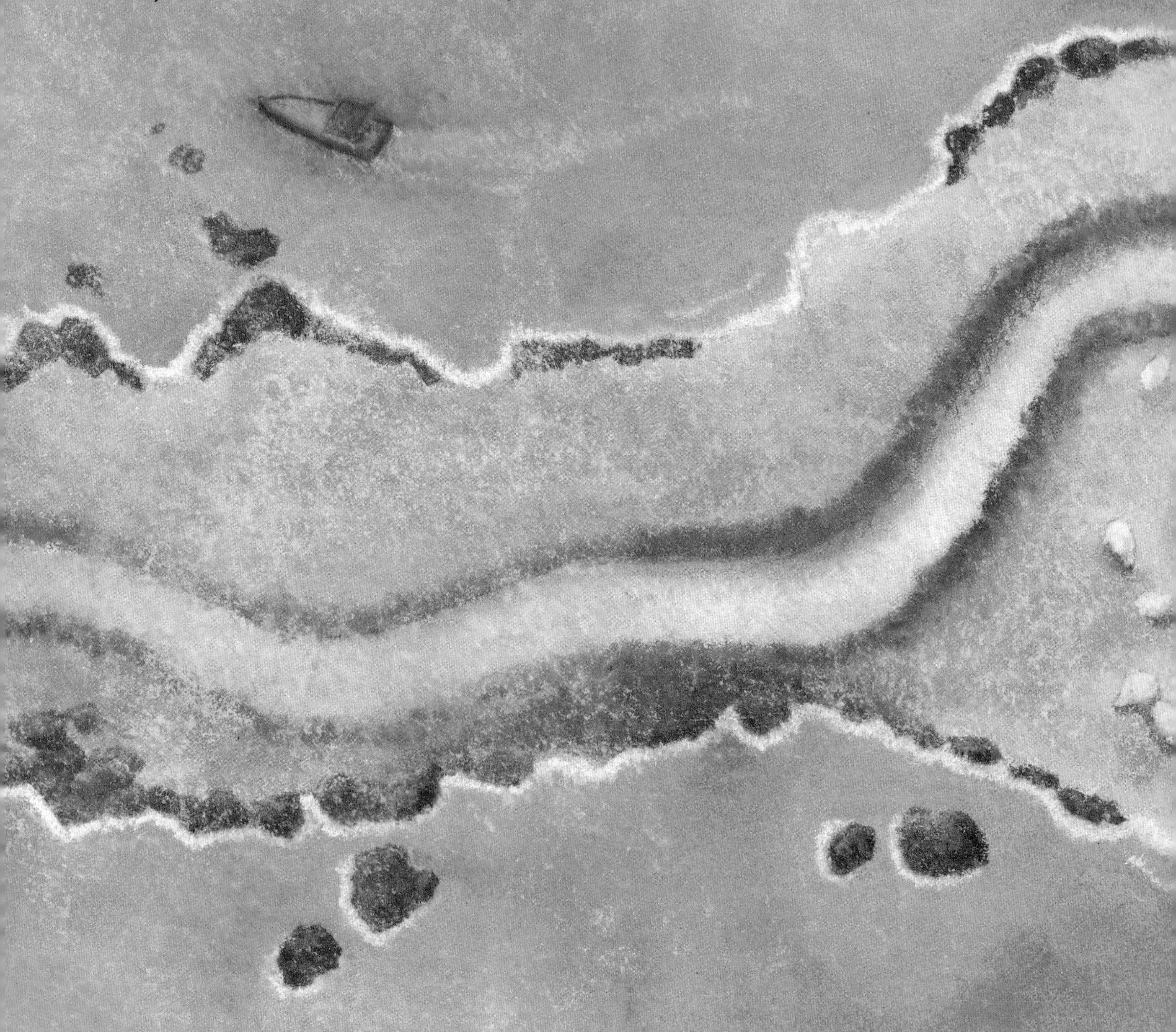

"'Is this the day?' I thought.
'Is this the one?'"

*"Gulls followed us, wheeling and calling,
diving into the wind as if it was water."*

"I couldn't wait any longer -
so we stopped the car and
I dialled the hospital again."

"Was it the day?" asked Jamie.
"The day that I was born?"
Aunt Isabel smiled.

"And this time, finally, they put
your mum on the phone.
'Well,' your mum said, 'he's here.
And we're just getting to know each other.'"

"'Yippee!' I called out to your uncle.
'He's here!'"

"That was me?" Jamie yawned.
"It was," Aunt Isabel said.
"Then what happened?" Jamie asked.

"And then," Aunt Isabel said,
"since we wouldn't get to see you
until the next day,
we drove to the edge of the land,
to the lighthouse that sits there,
waiting and guiding the ships in from the sea."

"We sat amongst the red clover and the heather,
and we sang out our greeting to you,
with seagulls turning and spinning overhead and
the water swirling in little dancing spirals, all of us singing for you."

"'Welcome to this day,' we sang,
'your very first one.'"

"You did that?" Jamie asked.
Aunt Isabel hugged Jamie tight.

"Yes," she whispered.
"We sat with the evening until it turned into night,
until the moon rose over us
and we fell asleep, dreaming of you,
shining too:
a new soul in this world."

All of a sudden, the phone rang out.
Aunt Isabel handed it to Jamie
and he heard his daddy and mummy say,
"Well, she's here! Your new baby sister.
And we're just getting to know each other."
"Yippee!" Jamie said. "She's here!"

And then, because they wouldn't
see her until the next day,
Aunt Isabel and Jamie
sat amongst their cats and their bedcovers
and sang out their greeting to her:

"Welcome to this day!" they sang.
"Your very first one.
Welcome."

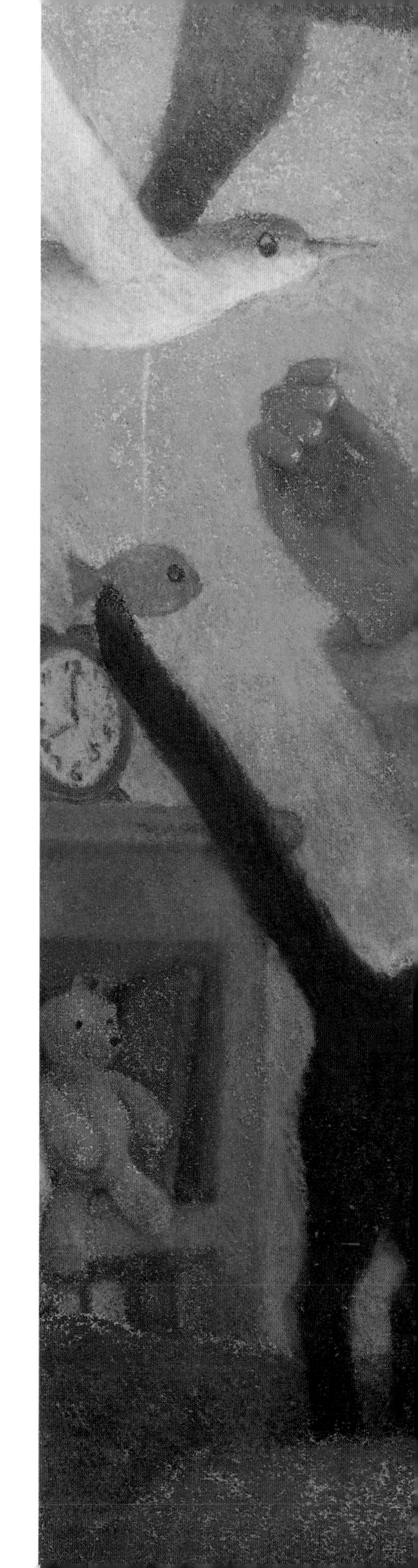

And then they turned out all the lights,
all over the house,
except for one –

Jamie's nightlight shaped like a seashell,
shining, just for her,
Jamie's brand new baby sister.